Chester Cricket's
Pigeon Ride

OTHER YEARLING BOOKS YOU WILL ENJOY:

YEARLING BOOKS are designed especially to entertain and enlighten young people. Charles F. Reasoner, Professor Emeritus of Children's Literature and Reading, New York University, is consultant to this series.

For a complete listing of all Yearling titles, write to Education Sales Department, Dell Publishing Co., Inc., 1 Dag Hammarskjold Plaza, New York, New York, 10017.

Chester Cricket's Pigeon Ride

by *GEORGE SELDEN*

Illustrated by Garth Williams

A YEARLING BOOK

Published by
Dell Publishing Co., Inc.
1 Dag Hammarskjold Plaza
New York, New York 10017

Yearling ® TM 913705, Dell Publishing Co., Inc.

ISBN: 0-440-41389-3

Reprinted by arrangement with Farrar, Straus & Giroux, Inc.

Printed in the United States of America

First Yearling printing—May 1983

*For Tom Andrews
Good friend to crickets, bees, beets—
and me!
G.S.*

Chester Cricket's
Pigeon Ride

Life in New York is very exciting.

It especially was thrilling for a cricket named Chester from Connecticut, who just two weeks ago had found himself in the Times Square subway station. It was there that he'd managed finally to free himself from a picnic basket. And then had been more or less adopted by two families: the Bellinis, who ran a newsstand, and a mouse and a cat named Tucker and Harry, who lived in an old abandoned drainpipe. So much happened to Chester during those first two weeks in the city that he could hardly believe he was the same country cricket who used to spend his days eating and sleeping and sunning himself on his stump in the country.

For a few days Mario Bellini, the boy who had found Chester his first night in New York, took him around and introduced him to everyone who

worked in the Times Square subway station. He met all the countermen from the lunchstands, the conductors on the Shuttle, the cleaning men who swept the station, and the three girls who worked in the Loft's candy store. And they all liked Chester. It somehow made them happy to think that there was a little insect from the countryside living right there in the heart of New York. He became the pet of the whole station. The countermen fed him, the conductors gave him free rides back and forth on the Shuttle, and the three girls saved him a chocolate cream candy every now and then.

But Chester didn't only stay in the subway station. One Sunday afternoon Mario took him to the Planetarium. Chester thought that was *awfully* in-

teresting! Back home, his favorite pastime had been stargazing. The top of his stump made an excellent observation platform, and he loved to come out and watch the slow drift of stars across the night sky. And in the Planetarium Chester recognized the same stars. They were showing a program called "Summer Nights." But all the changes that took place in a whole summer in Connecticut, the rising and falling of the constellations, happened in less than an hour in the Planetarium. At one point, when he saw a

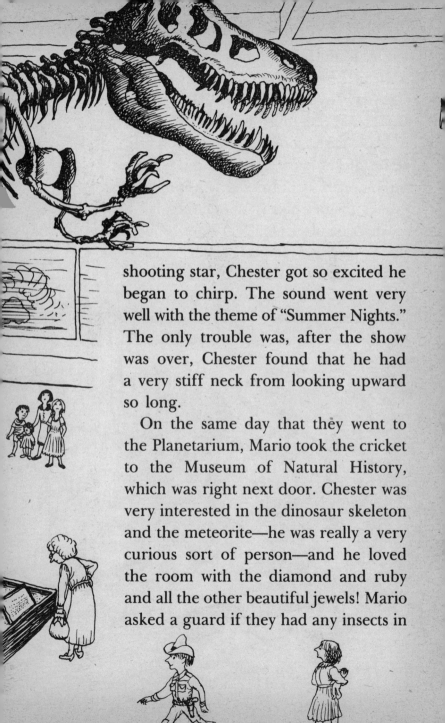

shooting star, Chester got so excited he began to chirp. The sound went very well with the theme of "Summer Nights." The only trouble was, after the show was over, Chester found that he had a very stiff neck from looking upward so long.

On the same day that they went to the Planetarium, Mario took the cricket to the Museum of Natural History, which was right next door. Chester was very interested in the dinosaur skeleton and the meteorite—he was really a very curious sort of person—and he loved the room with the diamond and ruby and all the other beautiful jewels! Mario asked a guard if they had any insects in the museum, and the guard said they used to, but that room was now closed. Chester Cricket really was glad to hear that. He didn't much want to hop along a glass case, looking down, and see some of his own ancestors pinned on little pieces of cardboard, with their names printed neatly under them.

And one afternoon Mario took Chester to his first movie. They sat in the balcony, and the boy put the cricket up on his shoulder so he'd have a clear view of the picture. The air conditioning in the theater was so cold Chester

had to wrap himself in Mario's collar to keep from shivering. And the movie itself made him very sad. It took place in the country, which looked for all the world like Connecticut. Chester was looking so hard at the fields and trees that he forgot to follow the plot. By the end of the show, he could almost have cried for homesickness.

The night after the movies, the Bellinis—Mario and his mother and father—went home early. Tucker Mouse and Harry Cat came over to the newsstand, as they did almost every night, to listen

to Chester's adventures of the day. Of course, going to the movies was nothing new to them. They would sneak out into Times Square and dart into a theater two or three times a week. Tucker knew more secret entrances—hidden holes and loose boards—than any other mouse in New York.

"Naturally I enjoy the films," Harry Cat said, and flicked his long tail around his forelegs. "But I really prefer the legitimate theater. For the past five years I've been the most eager theatergoer in New York. I've stood in the balcony, I've hidden backstage—why, once I even hung on a chandelier. There's nothing I wouldn't do to see a good play. Ah, the glamour—the romance of the theater! I love it!"

"That's nice," said Chester. "Have you been to many plays, Tucker?" He was still feeling blue, and didn't want to talk much.

"A few," the mouse answered indifferently. "I like musical comedies more."

"What a boor!" said Harry Cat.

"So I'm not a highbrow," said Tucker. "So what of it? Chester, you would probably like musicals, being a musician yourself."

"Maybe I would," said the cricket. But even the thought of music, which usually made him very happy, couldn't cheer Chester up now.

"We could go tonight," said Harry. "There's

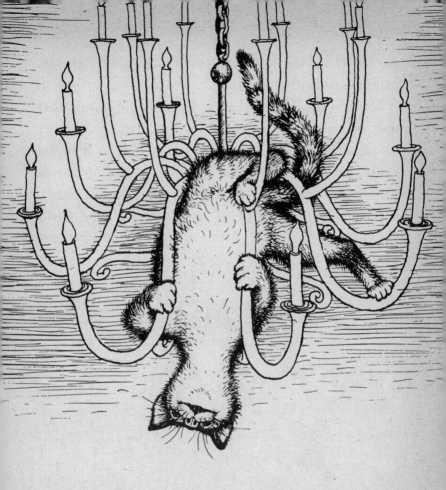

time to catch the second act of that new show that opened last week. It's just a little light review, but very enjoyable, I hear."

"Do you want to, Chester?" asked Tucker Mouse.

"Oh, I don't think so," said Chester. "Why don't you two go?"

"Is anything wrong?" asked the mouse. He suspected from the way Chester spoke that there was something bothering him.

"Not really," said the cricket. "But I don't feel like going out again today."

"Okay," said Tucker. He might not be a highbrow, but Tucker Mouse knew enough not to pry into other people's problems when they didn't want to talk about them. "Come on, Harry. Let's

you and me go. I could stand a little singing and dancing tonight."

The cat and the mouse told Chester good night, jumped to the floor from the stool where they'd been sitting, and went out the crack in the side of the newsstand. The cricket was grateful they'd gone. They were good friends of his—in fact, he liked them more and more every day—but there came times when a cricket had to be alone.

But now that he *was* alone, Chester didn't know what to do. In the mood he was in, he knew there was no use trying to sleep. Back in Connecticut, he would have jumped across the brook a few times, to tire himself out. He decided that a short hop was what he needed now. One leap took him from the shelf to the stool, the second to the floor, and the third out of the newsstand.

There was hardly anyone in that part of the station, and Chester could jump just where he pleased. He was bouncing aimlessly back and forth, when suddenly something above him caught his attention. It looked like some kind of light, but it shone with a soft, steady glow, unlike any of the lights Chester had seen in New York before. And then a cloud passed over it and Chester knew what it was: the moon, in its crescent. He was seeing the moon through one of the grates that led up to the street. And that made him even sadder, because it

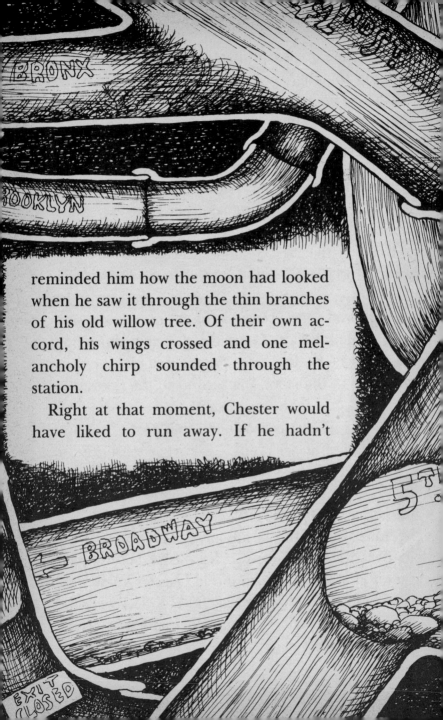

reminded him how the moon had looked when he saw it through the thin branches of his old willow tree. Of their own accord, his wings crossed and one melancholy chirp sounded through the station.

Right at that moment, Chester would have liked to run away. If he hadn't

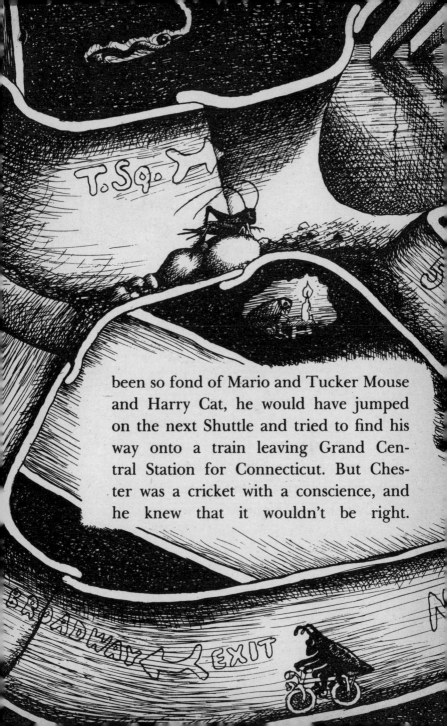

been so fond of Mario and Tucker Mouse and Harry Cat, he would have jumped on the next Shuttle and tried to find his way onto a train leaving Grand Central Station for Connecticut. But Chester was a cricket with a conscience, and he knew that it wouldn't be right.

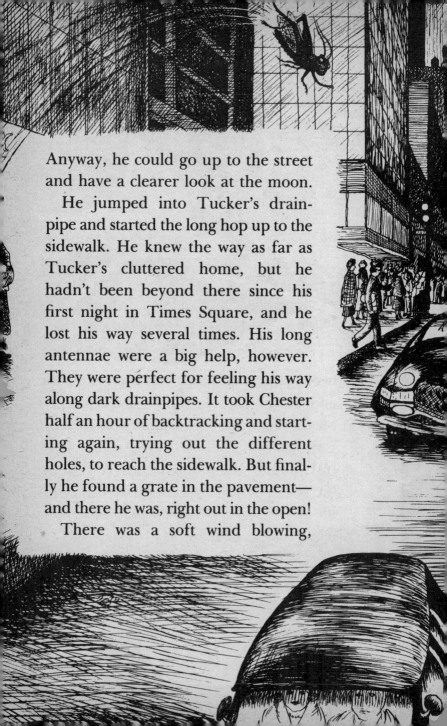

Anyway, he could go up to the street and have a clearer look at the moon.

He jumped into Tucker's drainpipe and started the long hop up to the sidewalk. He knew the way as far as Tucker's cluttered home, but he hadn't been beyond there since his first night in Times Square, and he lost his way several times. His long antennae were a big help, however. They were perfect for feeling his way along dark drainpipes. It took Chester half an hour of backtracking and starting again, trying out the different holes, to reach the sidewalk. But finally he found a grate in the pavement—and there he was, right out in the open!

There was a soft wind blowing,

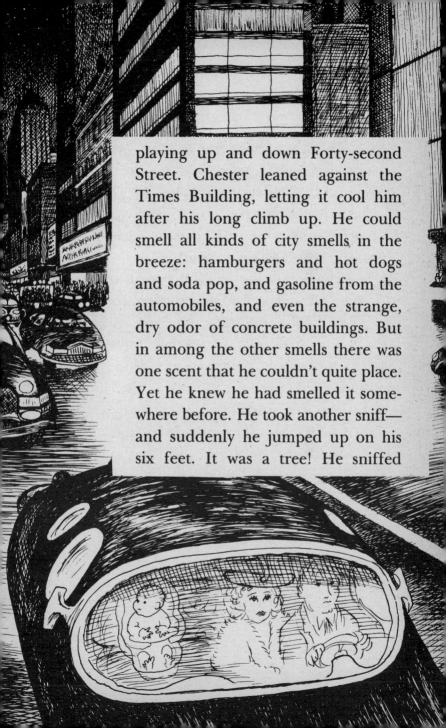

playing up and down Forty-second Street. Chester leaned against the Times Building, letting it cool him after his long climb up. He could smell all kinds of city smells in the breeze: hamburgers and hot dogs and soda pop, and gasoline from the automobiles, and even the strange, dry odor of concrete buildings. But in among the other smells there was one scent that he couldn't quite place. Yet he knew he had smelled it somewhere before. He took another sniff— and suddenly he jumped up on his six feet. It was a tree! He sniffed

again. And a sycamore tree at that—one of his fa-
vorites. He hadn't been near a tree for so long
he'd forgotten what one smelled like!

The sidewalk wasn't too crowded just then, so
he hopped out to the edge of the curb. Squatting
down, he collected his strength and then made his
highest jump into the air. But he still couldn't see
the tree. There was nothing but hundreds of bobbing headlights and human beings rushing back
and forth. It was down there, though, somewhere—he knew it. And he had to find it! Chester
had never struck off on his own in the city before,
but he couldn't resist. He felt that he'd be all right
again if he could just sit under that sycamore tree
for a few blissful minutes.

The best way to go, he decided, would be in the
gutter. That way he'd miss the people on the sidewalk and the cars in the street. The worst problem
was going to be getting across Broadway. He mea-
sured the time the light was green.

"About sixty seconds," he said. Sometimes it helps to talk to yourself when you're concentrating.

Then he stood up on his hind legs and tried to judge how far it was to the other side of Broadway. "Not more than thirty feet," he decided. "Now let me see. I can do three feet to a jump—so that takes ten jumps. And I *certainly* should be able to make ten jumps in one minute." So, by all his figuring, he ought to make it. But there wasn't going to be much time to spare.

He got on the very edge of the curb and flexed his legs, like a high jumper in the Olympic Games. This was by far the most serious jumping in Chester's whole life—and *much* more dangerous than crossing the brook back home.

The light changed.

He sprang out—a high arc—into the street. One.

He jumped again. Two.

There were human beings all around him, coming and going across Broadway. He had to keep going zigzag to miss them.

His third hop put him in the middle of the street. "May make it in only eight," he said.

But then something dreadful happened. A man who was in a terrible hurry cut into one of Chester's arcs. That's frequently what happens: somebody bumbles into your plans. Once the cricket had left the ground, he couldn't stop, and he hit the man right in the waist. The jolt stunned him and he fell back onto the asphalt. Luckily, there was no one coming behind him.

For a second, Chester couldn't think where he was. Then everything came back to him, but it was too late to move. The light had changed back to red. Headlights were rushing down on him from left and from right. Chester flattened himself on the street.

He was right in the middle, on the white line. Cars came whizzing by, in back and in front. One turned the corner and went completely over him. The wind from its tires almost tore him loose. But Chester clung to the white line with all his might. He didn't think that the light would *ever* change!

But it did. The cricket made three mighty leaps, and the last one landed him on the other side of the street. He crouched in the gutter, against the curb, panting. People were stepping over him onto the sidewalk, but Chester was safe. He hopped under a car and heaved a sigh of relief.

(Of course he couldn't know it, but he was the first cricket to cross Broadway since 1789, when it was still a country lane.)

Chester began jumping down Forty-second Street, following the smell of the sycamore tree. He had to make his hops low to keep from hitting the bottom of the cars that were parked beside the curb. Every so often, he would pass by the brightly lit entrance to a movie theater and a gust of cool air from the air conditioning blew over him. His mood of homesickness had changed completely. He was by himself, exploring—adventuring, in fact!—and he'd just crossed Broadway. He felt that if he could cross Broadway—well, he could do anything! Sometimes, just out of high spirits, he stopped and chirped a few times. But nobody heard, through the city's din.

Chester reached the end of the block. There was another street to cross—the Avenue of the Americas—but it wasn't nearly as busy as Broadway. And diagonally across from the curb on which he stood, Chester saw a remarkable thing: trees—and shrubs—and a fountain that dripped water into a marble basin. There was actually a little park, tucked away in the heart of New York City—and only a block from Times Square! He could see the sycamore tree—in fact, there were lots of them, arranged in rows, with cement walks between them. It was surely a sight to gladden a country cricket's heart.

As soon as the light changed, Chester launched right out into the street, ahead of all the human beings. When he got to the other side, he couldn't wait and crossed Forty-second Street against the red light. That is called jaywalking, and it is against the law. But Chester was so excited—and also so small—that no one saw him. And perhaps even the police wouldn't have minded if they'd known how eager he was to get to those trees.

The park was raised six steps above sidewalk

level. Chester took them two at a time, and his last
jump landed him—plop!—on real earth. It felt so
good to dig his feet down into it. For two weeks

now, he'd been jumping on concrete, on asphalt, and steel, but never on dirt. And it had made his legs quite sore. But now he was resting on the lovely springy soil itself.

The sycamore tree rose straight above him. He could see the moon again, riding through branches. A leaf fluttered down and landed beside him. Chester took a big bite out of it. And was it delicious! The sodas and liverwurst and chocolate candies were all very nice, but there was nothing like a simple leaf to suit a cricket's appetite.

Out of sheer pleasure in feeling the earth, and eating a leaf, and sitting outside in the night, Chester had to begin to chirp. The notes came

softly at first, and slowly, as if the cricket were test-ing the sound; but then more and more clearly they rang through the park. Chester was perfectly content when he sang. He could hear the chirping and feel his wings rubbing together, but he thought of nothing. A happy stillness filled his heart. Sai Fong, the Chinese gentleman who had sold Mario the cricket cage, had said that a cricket always sings the song of truth—the song of a per-son who knows all things. That may be so, but for Chester his song was simply the music of his de-light at being alive.

The song went on for several minutes. It was slow, then fast; then low, and then high. Like a thread of bright silk, it ran through the darkness. And then it ended. Chester never knew why a song ended. He could feel the end coming—and the music was over.

"Oooooo, my!" said a burbly voice behind him. "What have we here? A plump country cricket, I dooo believe."

Chester was so surprised—no, shocked—that he leaped in the air and whirled around. And there, standing in back of him, was the biggest pigeon he'd ever seen. It had a strange gleam in its eye.

Now, back in the Old Meadow, Chester had known several rather large birds. Beatrice Phea-sant and he got along very well. But there was also

Lou Blue Jay and Andy Blackbird, and Chester avoided them as much as he could. Because most of the big birds that he knew had one very special favorite meal: a nice plump savory country cricket.

"Um—er—" Chester stuttered. He didn't quite know what a person said when he might be gobbled up in a minute.

"That was beoootiful!" cooed the pigeon.

"You *liked* my song—?" Chester gasped, amazed.

"Groooovy!" the pigeon crooned.

'Well, for heaven's sake!' Chester thought to himself. 'I suppose I shouldn't be too surprised. If a cat and a mouse can live in a drainpipe, maybe me and a pigeon can also be friends.'

"I'm awfully glad!" he said out loud.

"More! More!" demanded the pigeon. "By the way, name's Lulu—" She pronounced it 'Looo-looo.' "What's yours?"

"Chester Cricket," said Chester. "But—um—er—let's get one thing straight. You're not going to eat me, are you?"

"Ooooo, goodness no!" and Lulu Pigeon laughed. "I only eat bread crumbs. There's the cuooootest little old lady who lives at the corner of 101st Street and West End Avenue. She has a shelf outside her bedroom window, and every morning it's loaded with bread crumbs—all for *me*!"

"That's very nice," said Chester Cricket. "Now"

—he was always a little embarrassed—"would you really like to hear another song?"

"I would love tooo!" enthused Lulu Pigeon. "Go, Cricket, go!"

With considerable relief, Chester chirped her one of his favorite songs.

"Man, that is the *greatest*!" Lulu exclaimed. "Now what is your *story*, Chester C.? How come you're singing down here in the city instead of out in the sticks somewhere?"

Chester told Lulu all about himself: being trapped in the picnic basket, and then found by Mario in the subway station, and then being "adopted," as you might say, by Tucker Mouse and Harry Cat.

"Dooo all the crickets in Connecticut sound like that?" asked Lulu, bobbing her head in disbelief.

"Oh, I don't know," answered Chester bashfully. As a matter of fact, he'd been told by a well-traveled robin named John that he was the finest musician in the state, but that wasn't the kind of thing you would tell a complete stranger.

"Now, what about *you*?" he asked, when he'd finished his own strange tale.

"Oh, me!" Lulu chortled delightfully. "I'm what yooo'd call a pecuoooliar pigeon. Or maybe even a kookoo bird."

Then Lulu told Chester *her* story. It seems that she came from a very old and aristocratic family of pigeons. In fact, her great-great-great—she couldn't remember how many greats—grandmother and grandfather, the Hynrik Stuyvesant

Pigeons, claimed to have crossed the Atlantic clinging to one of the yardarms of a vessel sailing to New Amsterdam. Lulu explained that that was what New York was called when it was still a Dutch city, before the English took over.

"They claimed they were 'bored' with the Old World and wanted tooo explore the New Frontiers," Lulu squawked derisively. "But I just think they couldn't make a living in Holland anymore."

Anyway, the Hynrik Stuyvesant Pigeons and all their descendants prospered greatly in the great New World. They became probably the most famous and respected pigeon family on the island of Manhattan—so famous and respected, indeed, that now they refused to eat any bread crumbs except those that were thrown out on Park Avenue.

"But about a year ago," said Lulu, "I had a beakful of all that ritzy jazz, so I told my snooooty relatives byebye and just flapped out. I decided that I'd rather, like, fly with the times. That's why I moved down here tooo Bryant Park. It's nearer where the action is. Yooo get what I mean?"

"I guess so," said Chester—although he didn't understand her completely. Lulu had a strange New York way of talking that was sort of hard to understand. But Chester meant to try, because he was beginning to like this pigeon very much. Even if there might be some kookoo bird in her.

Amsterdam 1650

"But don't you *ever* see any of your family now?" he asked.

"Oh, shooor." Lulu scratched the earth with one claw. "Every once in a while I fly up to Central Park. There's an elm tree up there reserved solely for the Stuyvesant Pigeon clan, if yooo please!"

"Where's Central Park?" asked the cricket.

"You don't know where Central *Park* is?" said Lulu. "Big, beautiful Central Park!—the best place in the city—"

"I guess I don't," Chester apologized. He explained that Mario had taken him on several excursions, but not, as yet, to Central Park.

"Say!" exclaimed Lulu. "How would you like a real tooor of Nooo York? One that only a pigeon could give."

"Well, I'd love one," said Chester, "but—"

"Hop on my back, just behind my neck. Nope—" Lulu bobbed her head jerkily, trying to think. "—Yooo couldn't see down through my wings too well." Then she gave a big scratch and exclaimed, "I got it! You sit on my claw—take the left one there—and wrap a couple of feelers around." Chester hesitated a minute or two. He was quite sure no cricket had ever done *this* before.

"Go on! Get on!" Lulu ordered. "You're in for a thrill."

"All right—" Chester mounted the pigeon's

claw, with a feeling that was partly excitement,
partly fear, and held on tight.

"First I gotta rev up."

Lulu flapped her wings a few times. And then—
before Chester could gasp with delight—*they were
flying!*

To fly! Oh, be flying!

"Sorry for the bumpy takeoff," said Lulu.

But it hadn't seemed bumpy to Chester at all.

"It'll be better when I gain altitooode."

Back in Connecticut, in the Old Meadow, when
Chester made one of his mightiest leaps—usually

showing off in front of a friend like Joe Skunk—
he sometimes reached as high as six feet. But in
seconds Lulu had passed that height, and in less
than a minute she was gliding along at the level of
the tops of the sycamore trees.

"Okay down there?" she called into the rush of
air they sped through.

"Oh—oh, sure—I mean, I guess—" There are
times when you don't know whether you feel ter-
ror or pleasure—or perhaps you feel both all at
once, all jumbled together wonderfully! "I'm fine!"
the cricket decided, and held on to Lulu's leg even
tighter. Because now they were far above even the
tops of the trees, and Chester could see whole
blocks of buildings below him. He suddenly felt all
giddy and free.

"How about a spin up to Central Park first?"

"Great, Lulu! I want to see *everything*!"

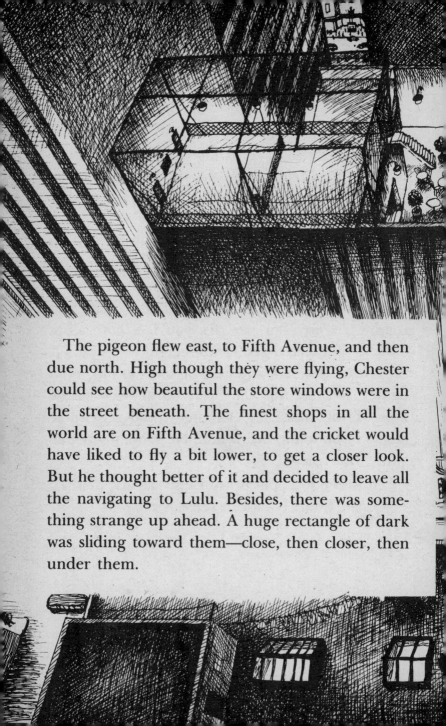

The pigeon flew east, to Fifth Avenue, and then due north. High though they were flying, Chester could see how beautiful the store windows were in the street beneath. The finest shops in all the world are on Fifth Avenue, and the cricket would have liked to fly a bit lower, to get a closer look. But he thought better of it and decided to leave all the navigating to Lulu. Besides, there was something strange up ahead. A huge rectangle of dark was sliding toward them—close, then closer, then under them.

"Here's Central Park," Lulu screeched against the wind.

And now Chester had another thrill. For there weren't only sycamore trees in the park. The cricket could smell birches, beeches, and maples—elms, oaks—almost as many kinds of trees as Connecticut itself had to offer. And there was the moon!—the crescent moon—reflected in a little lake. Sounds, too, rose up to him: the shooshing of leaves, the nighttime countryside whispering of insects and little animals, and—best of all—a brook that was arguing with itself, as it splashed over rocks. The miracle of Central Park, a sheltered wilderness in the midst of the city, pierced Chester Cricket's heart with joy.

"Oh, can we go down?" he shouted up. "Lulu?—please!"

"'Course, Chester C." The pigeon slowed and tilted her wings. "Anything you want. But let's not call on my relatives. They're a drag, and they're all asleep by now anyway."

"I don't want to *visit* anybody!" said Chester as Lulu Pigeon coasted down through the air, as swiftly and neatly and accurately as a little boy's paper airplane, and landed beside the lake. "All I want is—is—" He didn't know how to say it exactly, but all Chester wanted was to sit beside that shimmering lake—a breeze ruffled its surface—

and look at the jiggling reflection of the moon, and enjoy the sweet moisture and the tree-smelling night all around him.

And chirp. Above all, Chester wanted to chirp. Which he did, to his heart's content. And to Lulu Pigeon's heart's content, too.

But even the loveliest intervals end.

Song done—one moment more of silent delight—and then Lulu said, "Come on, Chester C., let me show you some more of my town"—by which she meant New York.

"Okay," said Chester, and climbed on her claw again.

"I want you to see it *all* now!" said Lulu. Her wings were beating strongly, rhythmically. "And the best place for that is the Empire State Building."

They rose higher and higher. And the higher they went, the more scared Chester got. Flying up

Fifth Avenue had been fun as well as frightening, but now they were heading straight for the top of one of the tallest buildings in all the world.

Chester looked down—the world swirled beneath him—and felt as if his stomach had turned over. Or maybe his brain had turned around. But something in him felt queasy and dizzy. "Lulu—" he began anxiously, "I think—"

"Just hold on tight!" Lulu shouted down. "And trust in your feathered friend!"

What Chester had meant to say was that he was afraid he was suffering from a touch of acrophobia—fear of heights. (And perched on a pigeon's claw, on your way to the top of the Empire State, is not the best place to find that you are afraid of great heights.) But even if Lulu hadn't interrupted, the cricket couldn't have finished his sentence. His words were forced back into his throat. For the wind, which had been just a breeze

beside the lake, was turning into a raging gale as they spiraled upward, around the building, floor past floor, and approached their final destination: the television antenna tower on the very top.

And they made it! Lulu gripped the pinnacle of the TV antenna with both her claws, accidentally pinching one of Chester's legs as she did so. The whole of New York glowed and sparkled below them.

Now, it is strange, but it is true, that although there are many mountains higher than even the tallest buildings, and airplanes can fly much higher than mountains, *nothing* ever seems quite so high as a big building that's been built by men. It suggests our own height to ourselves, I guess.

Chester felt as if not only a city but the entire world was down there where he could look at it. He almost couldn't see the people. 'My gosh!' he thought. 'They look just like bugs.' And he had to laugh at that: like bugs—perhaps crickets—moving up and down the sidewalks. And the cars, the

buses, the yellow taxis, all jittered along like miniatures. He felt that kind of spinning sensation inside his head that had made him dizzy on the way up. But he refused to close his eyes. It was too much of an adventure for that.

"Lulu, my foot," said Chester, "you're stepping on it. Could you please—"

"Ooo, I'm sorry," the pigeon apologized. She lifted her claw.

And just at that moment, two bad things happened. The first was, Chester caught sight of an airplane swooping low to land at LaGuardia Airport across the East River. The dip of it made his dizziness worse. And the second—worse yet—a sudden gust of wind sprang up, as if a hand gave them both a push. Lulu almost fell off the Empire State.

Lulu *almost* fell off—but Chester *did*! In an instant his legs and feelers were torn away from the pigeon's leg, and before he could say, 'Old

Meadow, farewell!' he was tumbling down through the air. One moment the city appeared above him—that meant that he was upside down; then under him—he was right side up; then everything slid from side to side.

He worked his wings, tried to hold them stiff to steady himself—no use, no use! The gleeful wind was playing with him. It was rolling him, throwing him back and forth, up and down, as a cork is tossed in the surf of a storm. And minute by minute, when he faced that way, the cricket caught glimpses of the floors of the Empire State Building plunging upward as he plunged down.

Despite his panic, his mind took a wink of time off to think: 'Well, *this* is something that can't have happened to many crickets before!' (He was right, too—it hadn't. And just at that moment Chester wished that it wasn't happening to *him*.)

He guessed, when New York was in the right place again, that he was almost halfway down. The people were looking more and more like people—he heard the cars' engines—and the street and the sidewalk looked *awfully* hard! Then—

Whump! He landed on something both hard and soft. It was hard inside, all muscles and bones, but soft on the surface—feathers!

"Grab on!" a familiar voice shouted. "Tight! Tighter! That's it."

Chester gladly did as he was told.

"*Whooooey!*" Lulu breathed a sigh of relief. "Thought I'd never find you. Been around this darn building at least ten times."

Chester wanted to say 'Thank you, Lulu,' but he was so thankful he couldn't get one word out till they'd reached a level where the air was friendly and gently buoyed them up.

But before he could even open his mouth, the pigeon—all ready for another adventure—asked eagerly, "Where now, Chester C.?"

"I guess I better go back to the drainpipe, Lulu. I'm kind of tired."

"Aw, no—!" complained Lulu, who'd been having fun.

"You know, I'm really not all that used to getting blown off the Empire State Building—"

"Oh, all right," said the pigeon. "But first there's one thing you *gotta* see!"

Flying just below the level of turbulent air—good pilot that she was—Lulu headed south, with Chester clinging to the back of her neck. He felt much safer up there, and her wings didn't block out as much of the view as they'd thought. He wanted to ask where they were going, but he sensed from the strength and regularity of her wingbeats that it was to be a rather long flight.

And the wind was against them too, which made the flying more difficult. Chester held his peace, and watched the city slip beneath them.

They reached the Battery, which is that part of lower New York where a cluster of skyscrapers rise up like a grove of steel trees. But Lulu didn't stop there.

With a gasp and an even tighter hold on her feathers, Chester realized that they'd flown right over the end of Manhattan. There was dark churning water below them. And this was no tame little lake, like the one in Central Park. It was the great deep wide bay that made New York such a mighty harbor. But Lulu showed no sign whatsoever of slowing. Her wings, like beautiful trustworthy machines, pumped on and on and on and on.

At last, Chester saw where the pigeon was heading. On a little island off to the right, Chester made out the form of a very big lady. Her right hand was holding something up. Of course it was the Statue of Liberty, but Chester had no way of knowing that. In the Old Meadow in Connecticut he never had gone to school—at least not to a school where the pupils used books. His teacher back there had been Nature herself.

Lulu landed at the base of the statue, puffing and panting to get back her breath. She told him a little bit about the lady—a gift from the country of France, it was, and very precious to America—but she hadn't flown him all that way just to give him a history lesson.

"Hop on again, Chester C.!" she commanded—and up they flew to the torch that the lady was holding. Lulu found a perch on the north side of it, so the wind from the south wouldn't bother them.

"Now, just look around!" said Lulu proudly, as if all of New York belonged to her. "And don't anybody ever tell *this* pigeon that there's a more beautiful sight in the world."

Chester did as he was told. He first peered behind. There was Staten Island. And off to the left, New Jersey. To the right, quite a long way away, was Brooklyn. And back across the black water,

with a dome of light glowing over it, the heart of the city—Manhattan.

And bridges! Bridges everywhere—all pricked out with tiny lights on their cables—that joined the island to the lands all round.

"Oh, wow! We're in luck!" exclaimed Lulu. With a flick of her wing, she gestured down. Almost right below them, it seemed, an ocean liner was gliding by, its rigging, like the bridges, strung with hundreds of silver bulbs.

An airplane passed over them. And even *it* had lights on its wings!

Through his eyes, Chester's heart became

flooded with wonder. "It's like—it's like a dream of a city, at night."

"You wait till I fly you back," said the pigeon. "You'll see how that dream can turn real."

The wind, which had been a hindrance before, was a help now. Lulu coasted almost all the way back to Manhattan, only lifting a wing now and

then to keep them on an even keel. But once or twice, just for the fun of it, she tilted her wings without warning. They zoomed up, fast—then dipped down, faster—a roller coaster in the empty air.

And all the while the dream city drew nearer. It seemed to Chester like some huge spiderweb. The streets were the strands, all hung with multi-colored lights. "Oh, Lulu, it's—I don't know—it's—"

"Hush!" said the pigeon. "Just look and enjoy." They were flying amid the buildings now. "Enjoy, and remember."

Chester Cricket could not contain himself. He gave a chirp—not a song, just one chirp—but that single chirp said, "I love this! *I love it!*"

Then there was Times Square, erupting with colors. Chester pointed out the grating he'd come through—and Lulu landed next to it.

"How *can* I ever thank you?" said Chester.

"Don't bother, Chester C. Just glad to meet someone who loves New York as much as I do. And come on over to Bryant Park again. I'll be there—one branch or another. Night, Cricket."

"Night, Lulu."

She fluttered away.

Chester bounded through the grate and hopped as fast as he could toward the drainpipe. He hoped that Tucker and Harry were back. Tonight he *really* had an adventure to tell them!

MS READ-a-thon— a simple way to start youngsters reading

Boys and girls between 6 and 14 can join the MS READ-a-thon and help find a cure for Multiple Sclerosis by reading books. And they get two rewards — the enjoyment of reading, and the great feeling that comes from helping others.

Parents and educators: For complete information call your local MS chapter. Or mail the coupon below.

Kids can help, too!

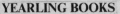

Judy Blume

knows about growing up. She has a knack for going right to the heart of even the most secret problems and feelings. You'll always find a friend in her books —like these, from YEARLING:

____ARE YOU THERE, GOD?
IT'S ME, MARGARET $2.25 (40419-3)

____BLUBBER $2.25 (40707-9)

____FRECKLE JUICE $1.75 (42813-0)

____IGGIE'S HOUSE $1.95 (44062-9)

____THE ONE IN THE MIDDLE
IS THE GREEN KANGAROO...............$1.75 (46731-4)

____OTHERWISE KNOWN AS SHEILA
THE GREAT $2.25 (46701-2)

____SUPERFUDGE $2.25 (48433-2)

____TALES OF A FOURTH GRADE
NOTHING..$2.25 (48474-X)

____THEN AGAIN, MAYBE I WON'T $2.25 (48659-9)

YEARLING BOOKS